ZELDA

the
QUEEN
of
BAD HABITS

Jim Schembri

Illustrated by
Gus Gordon

Supa
DOOPER.s

sundance
A Haights Cross Communications — Company

Published by
Sundance Publishing
P.O. Box 1326
234 Taylor Street
Littleton, MA 01460
800-343-8204
www.sundancepub.com

Copyright © text Jim Schembri
Copyright © illustrations Gus Gordon
Project commissioned and managed by
Lorraine Bambrough-Kelly, The Writer's Style
Designed by Cath Lindsey/design rescue

First published 1999 by
Addison Wesley Longman Australia Pty Limited
95 Coventry Street
South Melbourne 3205 Australia
Exclusive United States Distribution: Sundance Publishing

ISBN 0-7608-6628-7

Printed in Canada

CONTENTS

CHAPTER 1 An Almost Normal Girl 5

CHAPTER 2 Bad, Bad Habits 9

CHAPTER 3 School Time 19

CHAPTER 4 The New Girl in Town 29

CHAPTER 5 Sizing Up Darlene 37

CHAPTER 6 New Friends 41

CHAPTER 7 New Habits 51

CHAPTER 8 Amazing Discoveries 57

CHAPTER 1
An Almost Normal Girl

Zelda looked like a normal girl. She had normal hair, normal clothes, and a normal face. In fact, she seemed quite normal in every way.

But somehow, Zelda *was* different. She didn't want to be different. She just was.

Zelda wasn't different in a way that made everyone say, "Wow, Zelda! You're so different. You're so cool. We want to be just like you!"

She was different in a way that made everyone say, "Zelda, do you mind?" Or "Zelda, please stop that." Or "Zelda, be quiet!"

You see, Zelda was the most annoying person anyone knew.

CHAPTER 2

Bad, Bad Habits

She was annoying at home.

She was annoying at school.

She was annoying when she walked down the street. She was so annoying, it was amazing.

She was even annoying in her sleep. Zelda would snore so loudly that she would wake her whole family. They would come into her room and say, "Zelda, is that you snoring, or are you using a chain saw in here?"

Even when she was just watching TV, she was annoying. She'd whistle, or tap her fingers against the side of the chair, or hum to herself.

Sooner or later someone would tell Zelda to stop.

At the movies, Zelda would buy a box of popcorn. She'd make such a racket munching on the popcorn that the manager would come down and say, "Excuse me, Miss. Do you mind?"

14

15

Even if she sucked on the popcorn, people in the front row would turn around and say, "Hey, you! Keep it down! We can't hear the movie!"

Zelda couldn't even chew gum without annoying somebody. She chewed so loudly that people would cross the street just to avoid her.

It got so bad that the people at the store refused to sell her any more gum.

"It's not that we don't like you," they told Zelda. "It's just that you're so annoying."

CHAPTER 3
School Time

But school was the worst for Zelda.
She would be sitting at her table, listening
to what the teacher was saying. Suddenly,
the teacher would stop and say, "Zelda, do
you mind?"

And in 1916,
no Nobel Prize
was awarded
in physics.

Then Zelda would notice that she'd been tapping her pen.

Or clucking her tongue.

Or humming a TV theme.

One time, Zelda was asked to write the answer to a math question on the board. As she got up, her chair made a horrible scratching sound against the floor.

Some of the class put their hands over their ears. Others yelled at her. Some looked like they had just sucked on a sour lemon.

Even the teacher looked strange.

"Zelda, be more careful when you get up," she said. "I can't stand that sound!"

Zelda didn't have many friends. The other girls weren't being mean. Zelda knew that. Sometimes they tried to be friends with her, but something always went wrong.

One day, Zelda was having lunch with some girls. One of them told a joke while Zelda was drinking some orange juice. Zelda laughed so hard that the juice shot out of her nose like water from a kitchen faucet.

The girls were showered in orange juice.

"Ugh! Zelda! That's gross!"

"You *are* the Queen of Bad Habits!" said one girl. And they all walked off.

CHAPTER 4

The New Girl in Town

One day, Zelda was listening to the teacher. She was trying hard not to be annoying. Suddenly the teacher stopped and looked at Zelda.

"Here it comes," thought Zelda. "What's it going to be this time?"

"Darlene, do you mind?" said the teacher.

"Darlene?" thought Zelda. "My name's not Darlene. Who on earth is Darlene?"

The teacher wasn't looking at Zelda but at the table behind her. Zelda turned around and saw a new girl in the class.

Like Zelda, Darlene looked like a normal girl in every way. But right now, it looked like she was going to do something *very* annoying. It was much *more* annoying than anything Zelda had ever done.

Darlene was starting to put her finger right up her nose!

"What is it, Miss?" said Darlene.

"Well, Darlene," said the teacher, "you are doing something very annoying."

"Am I?" asked Darlene.

"Yes, you are. Can anyone tell Darlene what she is doing that is so annoying?"

Everyone put up their hand, even Zelda.

"Yes, Zelda," said the teacher.

"Darlene's putting her finger up her nose."

"Oh, am I?" said Darlene, who quickly took her finger away from her nose. Then she glanced around and made a rude face at the other kids.

"Darlene, get up and say you're sorry to the class," the teacher said.

"Yes, Miss," said Darlene. As she stood up, her chair scraped on the floor. "Sorry, everybody."

But nobody heard her. Some kids had their hands over their ears. One boy fell backward in his chair and hit the ground. And another boy jumped out of the window! (Luckily, he didn't hurt himself.)

Zelda felt very strange. Now there was somebody in the class who was even *more* annoying than she was.

CHAPTER 5

Sizing Up Darlene

At lunch, Zelda watched Darlene closely.

Some of the girls were trying to make her feel welcome. But it wasn't easy.

munch
chew
spit

Darlene spoke when she ate, and bits of food flew out of her mouth. She made so much noise when she chewed that the other kids almost needed to cover their ears.

Then someone told a joke while Darlene was drinking her orange juice. She laughed, and orange juice shot out of her nose like water from a firefighter's hose.

When Zelda had done that, she only sprayed the girls with juice. But Darlene knocked them onto their backs.

"Ugh!" they all said.

Zelda saw that Darlene wasn't going to have very many friends, either.

That night, Zelda slept soundly. This was very strange because her family usually woke her up to tell her to stop snoring.

CHAPTER 6

New Friends

The next day at school Zelda went up to Darlene.

"Hi, my name's Zelda. Do you want to be friends?"

"Why would you want to be friends with me?" said Darlene. "Everyone finds me so annoying."

"Well, I don't," said Zelda. "You're not as annoying as you think."

"But I'm more annoying than anyone," Darlene said. "I didn't have any friends in my last school because I was so annoying."

"I don't mind," said Zelda.

So they went to the movies. Darlene bought some popcorn and ice cream. She made so much noise slurping, chomping, and chewing, that nobody could hear the movie.

She opened a package of chips. It sounded like an asteroid had come crashing through the roof.

"Hey, you with the chips," somebody from the front row said. "Do you mind?"

After the movie, Zelda went to Darlene's house to meet her family.

They were all sitting on the couch in front of the TV. They seemed very friendly.

"This is my new friend, Zelda," said Darlene.

"Hello, Zelda," they all said. "Welcome to our happy home."

And it was a happy home, as far as Zelda could tell, because nobody minded what anybody else did.

Darlene's dad was flossing his teeth. Her mother was filing her nails. Her brother was munching from a big bag of chips. Her sister was plucking her nose hairs. And they were all having a really good time watching TV.

To Zelda, they looked like the most annoying family in the world—but they also looked like the happiest.

"Care to join us?" said Darlene.

"Don't mind if I do," said Zelda.

So Zelda sat down. She ate, and she burped, and she dropped her food. She was as annoying as she wanted to be. And nobody seemed to mind!

Later on, Zelda had to go home.

"It's so good to finally have a friend who likes me for just being me," Darlene said to Zelda.

"And you have such a lovely family," said Zelda.

CHAPTER 7
New Habits

The next day at school a funny thing happened. Zelda didn't do one single annoying thing. Darlene didn't do anything annoying, either.

In class they didn't tap their pencils on the table. Neither girl hummed or whistled or did anything annoying.

Darlene was asked to write the answer to a math question on the board. Everyone got ready for that horrible noise as her chair scraped along the floor. But it didn't happen.

"Zelda and Darlene, you haven't done a single annoying thing all morning," the teacher said. "Are you feeling all right?"

"We're fine," said Zelda with a smile.

At lunch, while Zelda and Darlene were drinking their orange juice, somebody told a joke. The girls took cover, waiting for the streams of orange juice to come shooting out of Zelda's and Darlene's noses. But it didn't happen.

That night, they went to the movies. They ate popcorn and ice cream and nuts. But nobody told them to be quiet.

CHAPTER 8

Amazing Discoveries

Zelda and Darlene found that all of their annoying habits just disappeared whenever they were together.

Life was easier for everyone—especially for them. They didn't have any more trouble at school, and they made many more friends.

And Zelda could watch TV with her family without anyone yelling at her.

The one place Zelda and Darlene *could* be annoying was at Darlene's house. But in Darlene's family, no one noticed because everybody was too busy doing their own annoying thing.

"Thank you so much for being my friend," Darlene told Zelda.

"It's me who should be thanking you," said Zelda.

ABOUT THE AUTHOR

Jim Schembri

Jim has been writing books since he was six years old, but it is only in the last few years that he has learned how to finish them. He has been a journalist since 1984.

The idea for *Zelda* came from memories of his early school days. "A lot of kids had bad habits, but it wasn't always their fault, and it didn't mean they were bad people. Some of them were very nice. They just needed a little understanding."

Jim lives with a cactus named Rodriguez that he waters once every leap year. His main ambition is to write a great novel someday.

ABOUT THE ILLUSTRATOR
Gus Gordon

Gus is a full-time freelance cartoonist and illustrator. He has drawn cartoons for many magazines and does advertising work for businesses. He loves illustrating kids' books, which probably has something to do with his inability to accept his age as fact!

He also teaches cartooning at schools throughout Australia and serves as Deputy President of the Australian Black and White Artists' Club, the oldest cartooning club in the world.

When he's not drawing, Gus enjoys surfing, diving, and reading books with lots of pictures.